EGMONT

We bring stories to life

First published in Great Britain in 2008 by Dean,
an imprint of Egmont UK Limited
239 Kensington High Street, London W8 6SA

Thomas the Tank Engine & Friends™

CREATED BY BRITT ALLCROFT

Based on the Railway Series by the Reverend W Awdry
© 2008 Gullane (Thomas) LLC. A HIT Entertainment company.
Thomas the Tank Engine & Friends and Thomas & Friends are trademarks of Gullane (Thomas) Limited.
Thomas the Tank Engine & Friends and Design is Reg. U.S. Pat. & Tm. Off.

HiT entertainment

ISBN 978 0 6035 6336 2
1 3 5 7 9 10 8 6 4 2
Printed in Singapore

Diesel and the Troublesome Trucks

The Thomas TV Series

The engines that work on The Fat Controller's railway love feeling Really Useful. But the Troublesome Trucks love being naughty and causing mischief. Sometimes they wear out the poor engines completely!

One day, The Fat Controller came to the shed to see the engines.

"Henry has broken down," he said.

"I have sent him to be repaired. I will use Diesel until Henry comes back."

"Yes, Sir," said the engines.
But they weren't happy.

The engines didn't like Diesel. He was very rude, and was always showing off.

"I hope Henry's mended soon," said Percy.

"He moves more trucks than three diesels put together," agreed Thomas.

"Trucks are nobody's friends," puffed Gordon.

The next day, Diesel was working at the Docks. "Wait till The Fat Controller sees how good I am," he boasted to the trucks. "He'll get rid of steam engines once and for all!"

This gave the trucks an idea.

As Diesel shunted the trucks together, they began to tease him.

"Can't you pull more trucks than that? Henry is much stronger!" they said.

Diesel was very cross!

"I'm stronger than Henry," snapped Diesel. "I could pull you all at the same time!"

The trucks giggled. "Pull us all! Pull us all! You'll be the strongest!" they chanted.

"That's me!" said Diesel. "The world's strongest engine!"

First, Diesel shunted five trucks together. Then ten. Then fifteen.

Soon, he had a long line of twenty trucks!

"What's Diesel doing?" asked Percy.
"He thinks he's the world's strongest engine,"
laughed Thomas.

Diesel got ready to pull the long line of trucks.
He pulled, and he pulled, and he pulled.
But the shunters had set the brakes on the trucks!

The trucks giggled. They tried to make Diesel pull them anyway.

"Pull! Pull! Pull!" they cheered.

Diesel pulled as hard as he could, but the trucks didn't move.

Diesel was determined not to give up. He pulled, and he pulled, and he pulled.
He pulled so hard that the couplings snapped.
Diesel shot over the quayside and landed on Bulstrode the Barge!

"Ouch!" moaned Bulstrode.

The trucks laughed, and laughed, and laughed.

Just then, Henry arrived back from being repaired. The Fat Controller was on board. He looked down at Diesel, crossly.

"I thought you would be as good as Henry, but I was wrong!" said The Fat Controller. "I'm sending you home."

The Fat Controller turned to Henry. "Can you make up for lost time, Henry?" he asked.

"Oh yes, Sir!" replied Henry, happily.

Henry backed up to the long line of trucks, and the shunters released the brakes. Henry pulled the trucks easily! All the engines tooted and cheered.

"Even Troublesome Trucks can be your friends!" laughed Thomas.

"Especially if they get rid of a smelly old Diesel!" puffed Percy.